When Spring Comes

BY Kevin Henkes

ILLUSTRATED BY Laura Dronzek

GREENWILLOW BOOKS

An Imprint of HarperCollinsPublishers

When Spring Comes

Text copyright © 2016 by Kevin Henkes

Illustrations copyright © 2016 by Laura Dronzek

All rights reserved. Manufactured in China. For information address

HarperCollins Children's Books, a division of HarperCollins Publishers,

195 Broadway, New York, NY 10007.

www.harpercollinschildrens.com

Acrylic paints were used to prepare the full-color art.

The text type is 32-point Bernhard Gothic SG Medium.

Library of Congress Cataloging-in-Publication Data

Henkes, Kevin.

When spring comes / by Kevin Henkes ; illustrated by Laura Dronzek.

pages cm

"Greenwillow Books."

Summary: "Animals and children alike watch as the world transforms from the dark

and dead of winter to a full and blooming spring"— Provided by publisher.

ISBN 978-0-06-233139-7 (trade ed.) — ISBN 978-0-06-233140-3 (lib. ed.)

[1. Spring—Fiction. 2. Seasons—Fiction.] I. Dronzek, Laura, illustrator. II. Title.

PZ7.H389Wh 2016   [E]—dc23   2014050050

16 17 18 19 20 SCP 10 9 8 7 6 5 4 3 2 1

First Edition

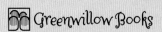 Greenwillow Books

For Will and Clara

Before Spring comes,
the trees look like
black sticks against the sky.

But if you wait,
Spring will bring
leaves and blossoms.

If you wait, Spring will make
the leftover mounds of snow smaller

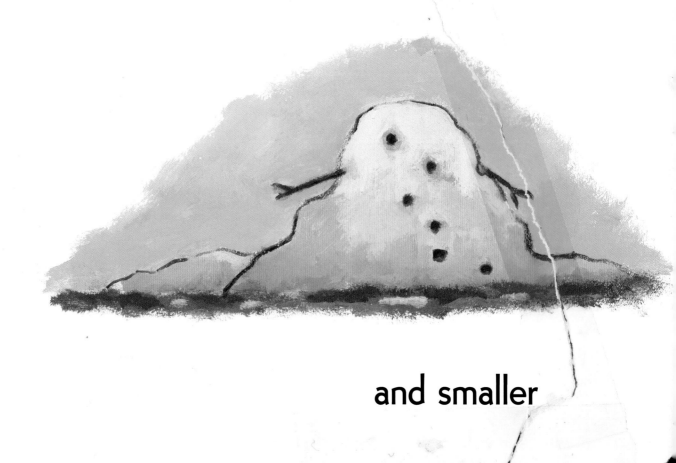

and smaller

and smaller

until suddenly—

they're gone.

Before Spring comes, the grass is brown.

But if you wait, Spring will turn it green and add little flowers.

If you wait,

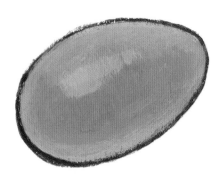

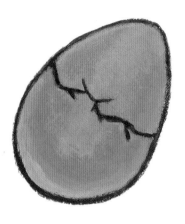

an egg will become a bird.

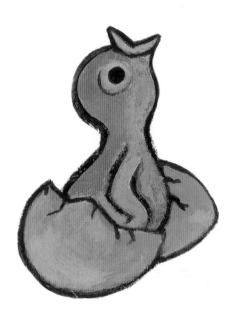

A seed will start growing.

Spring comes with sun

and it comes with rain.

And more rain

and more rain.

Do you like mud?
Do you like puddles?

I hope you like umbrellas.

Before Spring comes, the garden is
just dirt, and empty.

But if you wait, Spring will push green shoots through the dirt to fill up the garden.

And Spring will call out the pussy willows

and new kittens, too.

Spring can come quickly or slowly.

It changes its mind a lot.

But when Spring is finally here to stay,
you will know it. . . .

There will be buds
and bees
and boots
and bubbles.

There will be worms
and wings
and wind
and wheels.

You will feel it.
You will smell it.
You will hear it.

When Spring is finally here to stay,
you might think you are done waiting,
but you are not. . . .

Now, you have to wait for Summer.